My Reading Tree!

For my mother,
who doesn't like staying
in bed either!
~ M C

For Tony Downham
~ G W

LITTLE TIGER PRESS
An imprint of Magi Publications
1 The Coda Centre, 189 Munster Road, London SW6 6AW
www.littletigerpress.com

This edition published 2008
First published in Great Britain 1996

Ridiculous!

Michael Coleman

Illustrated by Gwyneth Williamson

LITTLE TIGER PRESS
London

"Ho-hum," yawned Mr Tortoise. "Winter is here."

"So it is," yawned Mrs Tortoise. "Come on, Shelley, time for bed."

"But I don't feel sleepy yet," said Shelley.

"*Ridiculous!*" cried Mr Tortoise. "All tortoises go to sleep for the winter."

"Why?" asked Shelley.

"Because it's cold outside and there's no food."

"But I don't want to go to sleep," said Shelley. "I want to see what winter is like!"

"*Ridiculous!*" cried Mr and Mrs Tortoise together. "Whoever heard of a tortoise outside in winter?"

Soon
Mr Tortoise
began to snore.

And not long after
that Mrs Tortoise
began to snore . . .

And not long after *that*, Shelley left her
warm bed of leaves, and out she went
through a hole in the shed to see what
winter was like.

Outside the shed, Shelley blinked.
There was snow and ice everywhere,
even on the duck pond and the hill.
As she lumbered along a duck spotted her.
 "A tortoise out in winter?" quacked the
duck.
 "Ridiculous!"

"No it isn't," said Shelley.

"Oh no? Then let me see you break through the ice to get food like *I* can. Ha-quack-ha!"

"He's right," thought Shelley. "I can't do that. I don't have a beak."

As Shelley began to walk up the hill,
she met a dog.

"A tortoise out in winter?" barked the dog. "*Ridiculous!*"

"No it isn't," said Shelley, feeling a bit cross.

"Oh no? Then let's see you keep warm by running around like *I* can. Ha-woof-ha!"

"He's right," thought Shelley sadly. "I can't do that either."

The dog ran off after a cat, but the cat jumped on to the branch of a tree. She looked down at Shelley.

"A tortoise out in winter?" miaowed
the cat. "*Ridiculous!*"

"No it isn't," said Shelley, even more
crossly.

"Oh no? Then let me see you run into
a nice, warm house as quickly as *I* can.
Ha-miaow-ha!"

"She's right," thought Shelley, shivering
with cold. "I can't run like a dog or a cat.
I'm much too slow!"

The cat raced off into her house
before the dog could catch her, and
Shelley trudged on up to the top of
the hill, where she met a bird.

"A tortoise out in winter?" cheeped the bird. "*Ridiculous!*"

"No it isn't!" snapped Shelley.

"Oh no? Then let me see you fly off home to cuddle up with your family like *I* can. Ha-cheep-ha!"

"Of course I can't fly," thought Shelley. "I can't even hop!"

Shelley felt cold and miserable. She
remembered her lovely, warm bed
and a tear trickled down her cheek.
  "They're *all* right," she thought. "A
tortoise out in winter *is* ridiculous!"
Sadly she crept behind a shed where
nobody could see her crying . . .

And slipped on a big patch of ice!
Shelley fell over backwards and
began to slide down the hill. Faster
and faster she went . . .

. . . faster
than a *dog*
could run . . .

faster than
a *cat* . . .

until suddenly
she hit a bump
and flew into the
air like a *bird*!

Wheeee! Down she came again and
landed on the icy duck pond. She
slithered towards her hole in the shed
but it was all covered up with ice!

"Ha-quack-ha, what did I say? Where's
your beak to break the ice with?" The
duck fell about laughing.

"I don't have a beak," thought Shelley.
"But I *do* have . . ."

"...a *shell*!"

And tucking her head inside it, Shelley smashed her way through the ice, into the shed and home!

23

Mrs Tortoise woke up as she heard all
the noise. "You haven't been outside,
have you, Shelley?" she asked.

"Outside?" said Shelley, snuggling into
bed. "Whoever heard of a tortoise out
in winter?"

And before you could say
"*Ridiculous!*"
Shelley was fast asleep.

Picture Dictionary

Look at the words below and put the correct picture stickers next to each word.

acorn   glove

jar   nest

paintbrushes   scissors

★ Have you put the stickers in the right place?
Then put a star on your reading tree!

Missing Words!

Oh no! Shelley has lost some of the words from the story! Can you help her? Put the word stickers in the right spaces below.

> winter – hole – bed – Outside – snow

Shelley left her warm _____ of leaves, and out

she went through a _____ in the shed to see

what _____ was like. _____ the shed,

Shelley blinked. There was _____ and ice

everywhere.

★ Did you get this right?
Remember to add a star to your reading tree.

Crazy Capitals

A sentence always begins with a **capital letter**.

E.g. **I**t is winter.

Capital letters are also used for **names** of people and places.

E.g. **Mr T**ortoise began to snore.

Look at the sentences below. Circle the letters that should be capitals.

1) as shelley began to walk up the hill, she met a dog.

2) the cat looked down at shelley.

3) shelley felt cold and miserable.

4) the duck fell about laughing.

5) mrs tortoise woke up as she heard all the noise.

★ Did you circle all the capital letters?
Put another star on your reading tree!

Drawing

Let's get creative! Draw a picture in the frame for each word below

tree	shed	leaves

★ Did you draw all three pictures?
Add another star to your reading tree!

Punchy Punctuation

A question mark (?) at the end of a sentence shows that it is a question.

An exclamation mark (!) at the end of a sentence shows emotions like surprise, excitement, frustration or anger.

Look at the sentences below. Write in a question mark or exclamation mark at the end of each sentence.

1) Whoever heard of a tortoise outside in winter

2) A tortoise out in winter is ridiculous

3) I can't run like a dog or a cat

4) Where's your beak to break the ice with

5) Wheeee

6) You haven't been outside, have you, Shelley

★ Did you find all the questions?
Let's add a star to your reading tree!

★ Did you find all the exclamations?
Then add another star to your reading tree!

Super Search!

Look at the picture below. Put the word stickers next to the correct objects in the picture. We've done one for you.

★ When you have put all the words in the right places, add the last star to your reading tree!